I0782208

Notes From No Telley Basin

The Mountain Wisdom of Huckleberry Henry

Volume 1

Edited by Phil Hudson

Publishing Services by BookCrafters
Parker, Colorado.
www.bookcrafters.net

Dedication

In memory of

Catherine

I'll see you up on
the Selkirk Crest
(7-5-1956 - 3-5-2023)

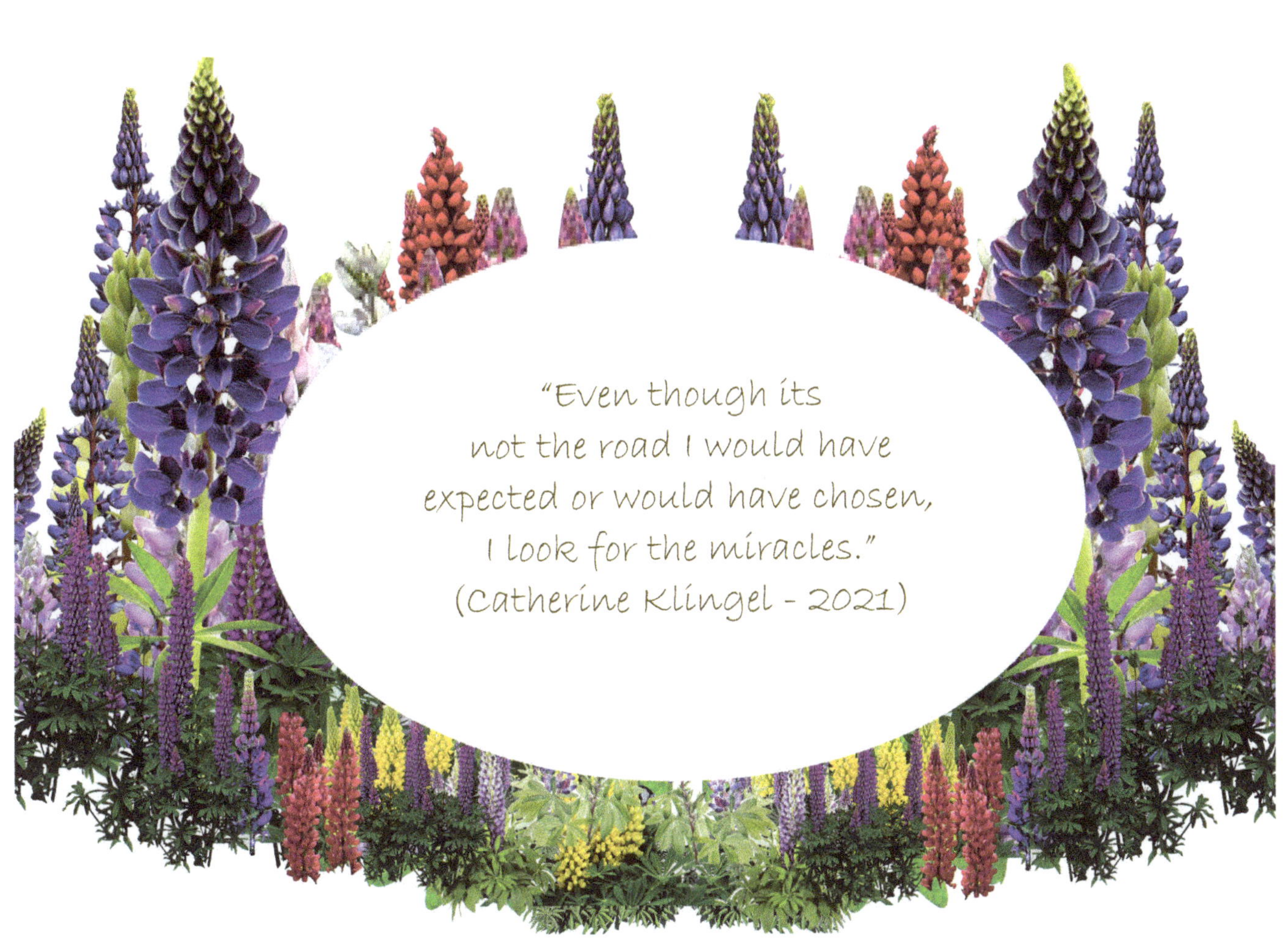

"Even though its
not the road I would have
expected or would have chosen,
I look for the miracles."
(Catherine Klingel - 2021)

Table of Contents

Foreword

For those of us who will take the time to listen, there is music in the mountain air, and at the end of each of Mother Nature's daily performances, we are reassured that, although in a coming day "the stars might fade away and the Sun herself grow dim with age, those who currently boondock through the wilderness in cadence with Her rhythms will flourish in immortal youth, and remain unhurt amidst the war of elements, the wreck of matter, and the crash of worlds." (Joseph Addison).

Perhaps you admire from afar the towering beauty of the Selkirks, or you may get down and dirty in its wilderness. Either way, there's no denying how mesmerizing the experience can be. From dealing with the fickle character of Nature to pitting your skills against whatever challenges life might throw at you, there are many ways that mountains can help shape your character. We have no limits up on the Crest where the air thins out and clouds meet the sky. It is there that we slip the surly bonds of Earth to top the windswept heights with easy grace. We tread the high untrespassed sanctity of our mountain home to touch the face of God.

Those who are engaged in a torrid love affair with the great outdoors, as well as those who enjoy only a casual platonic relationship with the mountain wilderness, are invited to turn to "Notes From No Telley Basin" to discover how Huckleberry Henry and those he admires have reigned in their raw emotions to creatively capture their inspiration in words. Their perspective will provide you with the literal and metaphorical tools to confront the mountains, as well as the molehills, that seem to loom before all of us with uncomfortable regularity.

Preface

You are sure to recognize the names of many of the luminaries cited in "Notes From No Telley Basin" and will doubtless already be familiar with some of their insights. But the real heart of the books can be found in the entries that have been paraphrased from the original text of the "Lost Journal of Huckleberry Henry." Each page contains delightfully different nuances on the mountain experience, contributing to a whole that is greater than the sum of its parts, and that represents a refreshingly egalitarian viewpoint. But make no mistake, without the rich wilderness flavor of Henry's contributions, any attempt to provide a comprehensive portrayal of the mountain experience in the stewpot of these volumes would fall short of expectations, and the resultingly bland fare would do frustratingly little to assuage the appetite for adventure of those for whom the wilderness holds a special place in their hearts and tummies.

As you leaf through the pages of "Notes From No Telley Basin", look for contributions from imposing intellects like Albert Einstein and Winston Churchill; from spiritual icons like Chief Seattle, Buddha, Lao Tzu, Spencer W. Kimball, and Mahatma Gandhi; from the creative minds of Robert Frost and Hans Christian Andersen, and from artists as diverse as Andy Warhol, Claude Monet, Ansel Adams, Vincent Van Gogh, Rembrandt, and Michelangelo. Look for the poignant observations of Anne Frank and Helen Keller, as well as the zealous admonitions of John Muir and Rachel Carson, and the transcendental exhortations of Ralph Waldo Emerson and Henry David Thoreau, the wise counsel of renowned explorers the likes of Edmund Hillary, Ernest Shakleton, James Cook, and Francis Drake, the measured jurisprudence of Oliver Wendell Holmes, the flowing prose of Robert Louis Stevenson, John Keats, Dante, Henry Wadsworth Longfellow, and Emily Dickenson, interpretations of visionaries like Frank Lloyd Wright, Leonardo da Vici, and Carl Sagan, the timeless counsel of Aristotle, Seneca, and Virgil, and the irrefutable logic of Edmund Burke, John Ruskin, and Voltaire.

But it is Huckleberry Henry to whom we must ultimately turn for a hands-on mountain perspective that has been forged in the refiner's fire up on the Crest, and then quenched in the icy cold waters of Priest Lake. As Hillary wrote of Shakleton, so could it be said of Henry: "For scientific discovery, give me Scott. For speed and efficiency of travel, give me Amundsen. But when disaster strikes and all hope is gone, get down on your knees and pray for Shakleton." In the Selkirks, if we were looking for someone to come to our aid and offer words of wisdom and welcomed succor, we would surely be overjoyed to see Huckleberry Henry appearing out of the mist as a benevolent apparition. It is for that reason that you are invited to enjoy these observations from his Lost Journal that have now seen the light of day in the two-volume set: "Notes From No Telley Basin."

Notes From No Telley Basin

(Volume 1)

Edited by Phil Hudson

When life feels like an uphill struggle, think of what the view will be like from the top.

"We are not in the mountains.
The mountains are in us."

John Muir

"Life's a bit like mountaineering.
Never look down."

Edmund Hillary

The climb is defined by our
character, but the view speaks
to our souls.

"If you truly love Nature, you will find beauty everywhere," but especially, I think, in the mountains.

Vincent Van Gogh

Time spent in the mountains is
action peaked adventure.

The most dangerous option
is to play it safe.

The summit drives us,
but it is the climb that matters.

We climb mountains so we can see the world,
and not so the world can see us.

The mountains that lie ahead of us
don't wear us out; it's the grains of
sand in our shoes that are often
in competition for our
attention.

"We need to risk going too far,
if we want to see how far we can go."

T.S. Eliot

It is one thing to decide to climb
a mountain. It is quite another to reach
the summit. And it's even more impressive
to get back down in one piece.

"Our peace shall stand as firm
as (the) rocky mountains."

Shakespeare

"What a glorious greeting the Sun
gives the mountains."

John Muir

Nature is our portal to
inner peace.

May your trails be crooked, winding,
lonesome, and dangerous, leading
to the most amazing views.

"In the mountains, you can lose your mind
and find your soul."

John Muir

A long life that is well-spent
is more important than getting
to the top of a mountain.

Edmund Hillary

No mountain is so tall
that it can block the Sun.

I have an appointment with
my therapist. Her name
is Nature.

If we want to accomplish great things,
we will need to find reserves of energy to
summit the mountains we will
encounter in our lives.

On big mountains, accidents
are more likely when ambition
has clouded good judgment.

Mountains have a way of
dealing with overconfidence.

We need mountains because elevators,
escalators, and even staircases
don't provide good hiking
opportunities.

Go to the mountains if you want to
flee demons or chase angels.

Climbing mountains is like hitting your head against a brick wall. It feels great when you stop.

Faith can move mountains, but you
have to keep pushing while you
are praying.

Three hikes
and you're out!

Mountains are
right up my valley!

When you are in the mountains,
you go from crags to riches.

Some view mountains as obstacles,
while others see them as a canvas.

"Mountains are not stadiums where we feed our ambitions. They are cathedrals where we practice our religion."

Anatoli Boukreev

"Mountains kindle enthusiasm, making every nerve quiver, and filling every pore and cell".

John Muir

"If you wish to experience the divine,
you need to feel the wind on your face
and the warm Sun on
your hand."

Buddha

"We don't inherit the Earth from our ancestors, we borrow it from our children."

Chief Seattle

"Never has Nature said one thing,
and wisdom another."

Edmund Burke

Find beauty in the mountains,
and you will be at one with
the mysteries of life.

Our achievements come from Nature, Who
is our Source and our inspiration.

"The mountains are
my altars."

Lord Byron

Nature is not a place we visit.
It is our home.

"Sunshine is delicious, wind braces us up,
rain is refreshing, and snow is exhilarating.
There is really no such thing as bad weather
in the mountains; only different
kinds of good weather."

John Ruskin

When you are in the mountains, let the
rain kiss your cheeks and caress your
shoulders with silver liquid drops.
Let its pitter and patter sing
to you in sweet lullabies.

The Selkirks
rock my world.

Mountain storms drive both trees
and people to send their roots
deeper into the Earth.

Hiking in the Selkirks will teach
you more than will googling
'Selkirks.'

"Heaven is over our heads,
as well as under our feet."

Henry David Thoreau

"The best thing we can do when
it's raining is to let it rain."

Henry Wadsworth Longfellow

If you google your symptoms when sick,
chances are you'll learn that the best
therapy is to get outside in the
fresh mountain
air.

"How strange that Nature does not knock,
and yet does not intrude!"

Emily Dickinson

"Wherever we go in the mountains,
we find more than we seek."

John Muir

The mountains cultivate our souls,
and if you look carefully along
the furrows, you'll discover
that the whole world is
one big garden.

"The poetry of the Earth
never dies."

John Keats

The mountains teach us how to live
in harmony with Nature.

One thing we all share
is our environment.

"We still do not know a thousandth
of one percent of what Nature
wishes to reveal to us."

Albert Einstein

Faith can move mountains,
while doubt can create them.

Boondocking in fresh mountain
air is the first step we take on
a journey to purify
our spirits.

"Nature does not hurry, and yet
everything is accomplished in due time."

Lao Tzu

If you're looking for me, you can
find me in the mountains.

"God wishes to see us happy amidst
Nature's simple beauty. I firmly believe that
it brings us solace in all our troubles."

Anne Frank

We don't conquer mountains;
we conquer ourselves.

"The mountains are calling,
and I must go."

John Muir

If you want to feel alive, come to North
Idaho, and then to the top of Highway 57,
where the pavement ends and
the adventure begins.

Aching feet are soothed by the
plush feel of a good pair of hiking boots.

Sometimes, we need a little less attitude and a little more altitude. We can shed the one and find the other in the mountains.

"Going to the mountains
is like going home."

John Muir

If you think you've peaked,
find a new mountain to climb.

When hiking in the mountains,
be sure to pack a light heart.

Go wild
in North Idaho.

"In all things Nature, there
is something of the marvelous."

Aristotle

Without fresh mountain air, the
still waters of a pool along a wilderness
creek, a crackling campfire to warm our
aching muscles, and peace and quiet, our
lives are incomplete.

Very little growth occurs on the
top of a mountain. Don't linger
too long at the summit.

If mountains could somehow be shielded from
the ravages of time, we would be denied the
example of the bristlecone pine, that has
managed to survive by learning how
to die very slowly and
elegantly.

"Those who contemplate the beauty of the Earth find reserves of strength that will endure as long as life lasts."

Rachel Carson

Somewhere within an old growth forest
of ancient western red cedar lies
the portal to a new world.

"The clearest way into the universe is
through a forest wilderness."

John Muir

"The Amen of Nature is
always a flower."

Oliver Wendell Holmes, Sr.

There is something about mountains that
wonderfully changes and renews our
weary spirits.

Solitary trees, if they grow
at all, grow strong.

Winston Churchill

"Nature is the source of all
true knowledge."

Leonardo Da Vinci

The weather can be fickle when
you are bushwhacking thru
the mountains, so bring
along your own
sunshine.

Nature is a source of solace, inspiration, adventure, and delight. It is not only a great teacher but also a wonderful traveling companion.

"To forget how to dig the Earth and tend
the soil is to forget ourselves."

Mahatma Gandhi

"Look deep into Nature to understand everything better."

Albert Einstein

There are no shortcuts to anywhere
that is worth hiking to.

When the Selkirks call,
mount me in.

"The planets are all dependent upon a Sun
that can still ripen a bunch of grapes
as if it had nothing else to do
in the universe."

Galileo Galilei

"Men argue,
but Nature acts."

Voltaire

The two doctors I have on call at all times
are my left leg and my right leg.

"Having land and not ruining it
is the most beautiful work of art that
anybody could want."

Andy Warhol

"The woods are lovely, dark, and deep.
But I have promises to keep, and
miles to go before I sleep."

Robert Frost

It's hard to get lost when you're on top
of a mountain. It's when you're in
the valleys that you can easily
get disoriented.

You'll need special shoes when you go
hiking in the mountains, and
an exceptional soul, as well.

Backpackers sometimes carry double the
amount of gear they'll need for half
the distance they planned to go
in twice the time it should
have taken.

If your path has no obstacles,
it probably doesn't go anywhere.

The weeds by the side of the trail
are just flowers in disguise.

If you're going through hell, join the club
and keep on climbing.

Welcome to the Selkirks. Be sure to
set your watch back 20 years.

After you've been in the mountains
for a while, you may grow beyond
the puzzle, and feel that your
piece no longer fits
the mold.

"The best way out (of the mountains)
is always through" them.

Robert Frost.

It's hard to walk in the woods and
remain in a bad mood.

If you've chosen not to climb the mountains
that loom before you, remember that the
absence of pain is the thief of life.

Walking is the most ancient exercise,
but is now the best modern exercise.

"In the mountains, we see that Nature always wears the colors of the Spirit."

Ralph Waldo Emerson

After a morning walk, everything
assumes twice its previous value.

We move through the mountains
with an easy grace, and not from a
noxious tankful of fossil fuels.

Hiking isn't for everyone. Have
you ever noticed how empty
the wilderness is?

If the winter feels uncomfortably cold and
the summer seems too hot, you may
be in the Selkirks, but you're not
yet a hiker.

"The secret of being your best is to grow in
the open air and to eat and sleep
with the Earth."

Walt Whitman

"It doesn't matter how slowly you go,
as long as you don't stop."

Confucius

The summit is not the
finish line.

In the mountains, carry as little as possible,
but choose that little very carefully.

Remember to turn everything off once a week, including your troubled spirit, and then to walk quietly in the mountains.

Think outside.
No box required.

"I went to the woods because I wished
to see if I could learn what they had to
teach me, and not, when I came to die,
to discover that I had not lived."

Henry David Thoreau

"Mountains are my life, my work,
and it is too late for me to
follow another path."

Anatoli Boukreev

(1958 – 12/25/1997)

Hikes in the mountains
walk our souls back home.

We go to Nature to be soothed and healed,
and to have our senses recalibrated.

Hiking in the mountains
can be a hill of a lot of fun.

The next time you're tramping through a
mountain meadow, remember that
a leaf of grass is no less than the
work of the stars."

Walt Whitman

We don't see Nature with our eyes,
but with our hearts.

In the Selkirks, try not to
take hiking for granite.

To sit in the shade" upon our
return from the mountains, "and
to look upon verdure, is the most
perfect refreshment."

Jane Austen

It's a hill -
get over it.

"Walking
is the best medicine."

Hippocrates

North Idaho: Fresh air and
fond memories served daily.

Those who find themselves wandering among big trees are simply returning to their roots.

Sleeping bags are the
soft tacos of the bear world.

"All truly great thoughts
are conceived when walking."

Friedrich Nietzsche

If you hike like a girl, the question is:
Will others will be able to keep up?

When you're in the mountains, it
feels good to be lost, as long as you're
headed in the right direction.

Wander
where the WiFi is weak.

Nature
is the art of God.

Dante Alighieri

Happy trails lead to the 4 cardinal points
of the compass, as well as to the physical,
mental, emotional, and spiritual
foundations of our nature.

A day-hike in the mountains is the
best way to take a quick peak
around the Selkirks.

Real adventure is when you embark upon a journey in the mountains from which you may not come back alive, and certainly not as the same person that you were previously.

"No matter how sophisticated we may
be, mountains cannot be denied.
In silence, they speak to the
very core of our being."

Ansel Adams

When hiking in the Selkirks, "adopt the pace
of Nature, Whose secret is patience."

Ralph Waldo Emerson

After a few days in North Idaho,
we begin hoping that heaven is a place
where we never have to go, because it seems
that the Selkirks are greater than
any paradise could be.

When we are tramping
on soft forest duff in the
mountains, we can hear
the whispering of
angels.

"Preserve and cherish
our pale blue dot. It's the
only home we've ever known."

Carl Sagan

Get used to the fact that as you climb higher, the wind will blow harder.

We don't stop climbing because we
grow old. We grow old because
we stop climbing.

Without new experiences, something inside us is lulled to sleep. Sometimes, it takes a mountain to awaken a sleeping giant.

When you've taken a walk in the woods,
you come out taller than the trees.

The beauty of the Selkirks
is rock-solid.

Happiness and hiking go hand
in hand and feet in boots.

Hike more, and
worry less.

"Of all the paths you take in life,
make sure a few of them are dirt."

John Muir

Anywhere is within walking
distance, if you take the time.

"Two roads diverged in a wood, and I took
the one less traveled by, and that has
made all the difference."

Robert Frost

"I believe in
God, only I spell it
N-a-t-u-r-e."

Frank Lloyd Wright

"The journey of a thousand miles begins
with a single step."

Lao Tzu

"Into the forest I go, to lose my mind
and find my soul."

John Muir

"It's not the mountain we conquer,
but ourselves."

Edmund Hillary

"Do not follow where the path may lead.
Go, instead, where there is no path,
and leave a trail" for others
to follow."

Ralph Waldo Emerson

"Use what talents you possess. The woods would be silent if no birds sang there except those that sang best."

Henry van Dyke

"There is pleasure in the pathless woods,
there is a rapture on the lonely shore,
there is society, where none intrudes,
by the deep sea, and music in its
roar: I love not man the less,
but Nature more."

Lord Byron

If you're looking for the mountain
of youth, you might just find it
while tramping in the
wilderness.

"An early morning walk
is a blessing for the whole day."

Henry David Thoreau

DEET is
Nature's cologne.

"To me, a lush carpet of pine needles or spongy grass is more welcome than the most luxurious Persian rug."

Helen Keller

"One touch of Nature makes
the whole world kin."

William Shakespeare

I haven't been everywhere in the Selkirks,
but it's on my bucket list.

Keep going,
come hill or high water.

High up on the Crest, we always look forward to "a sunrise, a glitter of green and golden wonder in a vast edifice of stone and space."

Ansel Adams

"If you're not in awe of Mother Nature,
there's something wrong with you."

Alex Trebek

Hiking in the mountains may initially leave us speechless, but eventually, it will turn us into great storytellers.

"Choose only one master:
Nature."

Rembrandt

"There are always plenty of flowers
in mountain meadows for those
who want to see them."

Henri Matisse

Exploring the Selkirks is a wonderful way
to open our eyes, and to see that "impossible"
is nothing but a word that motivates
us to greater accomplishment.

If you're feeling low,
go to the mountains.

Every flower in a mountain meadow
is the blossoming of Nature's soul.

The path we must follow is probably going
to be uphill in both directions.

"Keep close to Nature's heart and break clear away once in a while. Climb a mountain or spend a week in the woods to wash your spirit clean."

John Muir

Even when you're out picking huckleberries in the mountains, you mustn't "judge the day by the harvest you reap, but by the 'seeds' you plant."

Robert Louis Stevenson

If there is no heaven on Earth,
surely we can at least find evidence
of it in the mountains.

Hiking can be better
than curling up with a good book,
even though, at times, it can seem like
climb and punishment.

When you're from Minnesota,
it's all aboot the mountain lifestyle.

"My wish is to stay always like this, living quietly in a corner of Nature."

Claude Monet

"The moment my legs begin to move,
my thoughts begin to flow."

Henry David Thoreau

"Procrastipacking" is thinking about organizing your 'possibles' bag without actually doing it.

When you are caught by evening high up
in the Selkirks, "do not go gentle into that
good night. Rage, rage against the dying
of the light."

Dylan Thomas

The mountains inflate our lungs
with the onrush of magnificent scenery.

In the mountains, "the Earth delights to feel your bare feet, and the wind longs to play with your hair."

Khalil Gibran

"Live in each season as it passes;
breathe the air, taste the fruit,
and submit yourself to the
influence of the Earth."

Henry David Thoreau

While hiking in the mountains, our pulse
rates quicken to bring us into harmony
with Mother Nature and match the
rhythm of the cosmos.

At the end of the day,
no-one visits the Selkirks accidentally.

In the mountains, if we listen very
carefully, Nature will open our ears
to one of the greatest stories
She has ever told.

"A glance at the mountains outside
my window satisfies me more than the
metaphysics of books."

Walt Whitman

"I wish the world were twice as big and that half of it was still unexplored."

David Attenborough

The mountains attract those who are
fed up with conventionality.

We find ourselves at one with the secrets
of life itself, when we discover the magic
of the mountains.

You should smell like sweat mixed
with dirt at the end of a long
day in the mountains.

"For most of history, we have
had to fight Nature to survive; in
this century we are beginning to
realize that, in order to survive,
we must protect Nature."

Jacques Cousteau

There may be no Wi-Fi in the mountains, but it is there that we will find a better connection.

If things are consistently going your way,
congratulations. You're on a winning peak.

Don't be sad if you've done something wonderful and nobody notices. Nearly every morning, Nature's sunrise is spectacular, and yet most of her potential audience have not yet opened their eyes.

If you're in the depths of depression,
get outside and climb a mountain. Maybe
you just need to change your altitude.

If you want to play hide and peak
with friends, head for the mountains.

The mountains generally begin
at the end of your comfort zone.

"All my life, the sights of
Nature have made me
rejoice, as a child."

Marie Curie

Hiking in the Selkirks
provides great opportunities for
us to mount our blessings.

There's no time for boredom
in a world with beautiful mountains.

"There is something infinitely healing in the repeated refrains of Nature, the assurance that dawn comes after night, and spring after winter."

Rachel Carson

Without mountains, we may be relieved
to have avoided the pain of the climb,
but we will forever miss the thrill of
the summit and the new vistas
that might have been ours
during the descent.

Confident people enjoy the journey even
more than first ascents, and they are
in competition with neither
man nor Nature.

Those who risk everything to reach the summit are half in love with themselves, and half in love with oblivion.

We hike in the mountains because we
seek adventure. Something inside
of us dies when we lose that
burning desire.

Don't sweat the
tall stuff.

"You're off to great places; today is your
day. Your mountain is waiting,
so get on your way."

Dr. Seuss

Afterword

Huckleberry Henry cuts to the chase, and tells it like it is, in "Notes From No Telley Basin".
Living up on the Crest, he knows better than most, that to each of us upon this earth, death
will come soon or late, but we cannot die better than facing fearful odds while challenging the
mountains for the ashes of our fathers and the temples of our gods. So, dear reader, use these
observations as fuel to be added to the fire of your resole. Carpe diem! As an addendum to his Lost
Journal, Henry included his own observations as gifts to be opened each day of the year. So, there
is no need to rush through them. They are meant to be savored, and leisurely turned over in our
minds, that they might nourish new perspectives on our wilderness experiences.

Maybe the next time you're up on the Crest, you'll encounter Henry on the trail, and have a chance to sit down with him and share a bit of rabbit from the spit, before heading your separate ways. If that is the case, as he fades into the shadows of the Selkirks, listen for his exclamation: ""I ain't never seen 'em, but my common sense tells me that compared to the Selkirks, the Andes is foothills, and the Alps is for children to climb! These here mountains is God's finest sculpturings! In the Selkirks, there ain't no laws for the brave ones, and there ain't no asylums for the crazy ones! And there ain't no churches, except for the mountains, and there ain't no priests, excepting the birds. By God, I are a mountain man!"

About The Author

Phil Hudson cannot take credit for this volume. Its insights into mountain life belong to Huckleberry Henry, and to him alone. It has been an honor for Phil to have been entrusted with the care and safe keeping of these entries that have been excerpted from his Lost Journal. He is humbled to have been an instrument in bringing them into the light of day, that the sphere of Henry's influence might expand to include all those who love tramping in the woods below the Crest. Phil feels that he has gotten to know Henry as he has read his Journal, and he hopes you will feel the same. He is certain that Henry would be pleased to know that his thoughts have contributed to an appreciation of the wilderness by so many of his friends at Priest Lake.

Within this two-volume set, many of the hundreds of illustrations depicting Huckleberry Henry were captured during chance encounters while Phil was hiking in the back country. Most of the time Henry remained unaware that Phil was taking his photograph using a long telephoto lens with a tripod, although there were occasions when he seemed to be staring right into the camera. Henry has not explicitly given Phil his permission to include the images that you have enjoyed in this volume, but as the caretaker of his Lost Journal, and given the unusual circumstances under

which it was found and has made its way to publication, Phil does not feel that their inclusion is a violation of Henry's trust. It seems to him that the quality of "Notes From No Telley Basin" has been enhanced by selected illustrations that are representative of Henry's life. However, to protect his privacy, Phil has chosen not to divulge when, or where, or under what circumstances, the photos were taken. However, friends of Priest Lake may recognize geographic features in the background that could provide clues to the locations of Five Mile Ridge, No Telley Basin, the Woodland Elves' Glitter Mine, and even Henry's cabin in the woods, all of which are frequently referenced in the companion volumes to "Notes From No Telley Basin."

230

Phil and his wife Jan have 7 children and 25 grandchildren, all of whom could relate to you chance encounters they have had with Huckleberry Henry. They enjoy spending time with their family at their cabin nestled beneath th Selkirk Crest, on the shore of Priest Lake, the crown jewel of North Idaho. He always finds time, however, to record his thoughts on his laptop, and understands Isaac Asimov's response when he was asked: "If you knew that you had only 10 minutes left to live, what would you do?" He answered: "I'd type faster." Phil received the inspiration to compile this volume from The Lost Journal of Huckleberry Henry as he sat on the beach at Northwinds and looked out over the lake at the imposing skyline to the north, punctuated by Mollies' and Phoebes' Tips, Trapper Peak, Green Bonnet, and Little Snowy Top. He realized that he had an opportunity to witness God's Country through the clarifying lens of his good friend's Journal.

You Might Also Like

The Strange Tale of Huckleberry Henry
Huckleberry Henry: The Lost Journal (Volume 1)
Huckleberry Henry: The Lost Journal (Volume 2)
Notes From No Telley Basin (Volume 2)

Parting Thought

When life gives you mountains,
make memories. Put your boots
on, go for a hike, and keep an
eye out for Huckleberry
Henry.

Up on the Crest

Sometimes, beautiful pathways can only be
discovered by first getting lost.

Up on the Crest

Sometimes, our faith is meant to
move mountains one rock at a time.

Up on the Crest

Hikers in the Selkirks during the spring
runoff are gushing with joy.

Up on the Crest

A hike in the wilderness reminds us that
Nature never goes out of style.

Up on the Crest

When the mountains whisper to us,
our souls respond to the call.

Up on the Crest

Our lives are calibrated by stars rather
than by clocks. Our engagement
with life helps us forget to
check our cellphones.

At the Wigwams

In the Selkirks, waterfalls wouldn't
sound so lyrical if there were
no rocks in the way.

At the Wigwams

"Nature is painting for us, day after day, pictures of infinite beauty, if only we have the eyes to see them."

John Ruskin

At the Wigwams

The creeks in the Selkirks are
streaming right now, on the
Nature Channel.

At the Wigwams

Paradise Lost. Paradise Found.
(In the Selkirks).

At the Wigwams

The trick to not getting swept over
a waterfall in the mountains,
is swimming against
the current.

At the Wigwams

The best gift you can give someone
you love is a lifetime of adventure.

Five Mile Ridge

You climb mountains with your feet, but you can only move them with your faith.

Five Mile Ridge

Those who love boondocking in the
Selkirks have learned that not
every paradise is tropical.

Five Mile Ridge

Through the misty breeze beneath
every waterfall, there is a rainbow
calling out to you.

Five Mile Ridge

Adventure is germinated within our
thoughts, catalyzed by our words,
and executed in our actions.

Five Mile Ridge

A thunderstorm in the Selkirks is
Mother Nature flexing Her muscles.

Five Mile Ridge

In the Selkirks, we trip on the sky
to sip from the streams.

On the trail to
No Telley Basin

Summer showers in the Selkirks
water our roots, so our souls can grow.

On the trail to
No Telley Basin

Adventure is the invention
of restless minds.

On the trail to
No Telley Basin

It is to the mountains that we are frequently invited, where we are often tolerated, and sometimes asked to go home.

On the trail to
No Telley Basin

I'd rather be in the mountains thinking of
God, than in church dreaming of
the mountains.

On the trail to
No Telley Basin

Sometimes, a leisurely hike in the
mountains means enjoying life
in the snow lane.

On the trail to
No Telley Basin

Waterfalls in the Selkirks
wink at every passerby.

No Telley Basin

If you find that your faith can't move a mountain, maybe it is because God meant for you to climb it instead.

No Telley Basin

The only way to know a mountain
is to live its four seasons.

No Telley Basin

In the Selkirks in the spring,
we learn to go with the flow.

No Telley Basin

Lion Creek has cut through thousands of feet of granite not because of its power, but because of its persistence.

No Telley Basin

May your dreams be larger than mountains,
and may you have the courage to reach
their summits.

No Telley Basin

We can never really get lost in the
mountains, because it is where
we go to find ourselves.

Elven Glitter Mines

Hiking in the mountains isn't a
tour, it's a tale of adventure.

Elven Glitter Mines

"To an illumined mind the
world burns and sparkles with light."

Ralph Waldo Emerson

Elven Glitter Mines

If your faith can't seem to move
a mountain, maybe you should
try persistence.

Elven Glitter Mines

At Priest Lake, many hikers fall in love with
its tumbling creeks quite rapidly.

Elven Glitter Mines

If you listen carefully to the sounds of
Nature, you will discover the voices
of life, being, and perpetual
becoming.

Elven Glitter Mines

In the mountains, "our minds become raging torrents, flooded with rivulets of thought cascading into waterfalls of creative alternatives."

Mel Brooks

Dreams of Nell Shipman

Throughout the Selkirks, when we hear
waterfalls, we are witnessing
Nature's laughter.

Dreams of Nell Shipman

When we are hiking in the Selkirks
during the spring runoff, we
are live-streaming.

Dreams of Nell Shipman

Adventure isn't hanging on a rope off
the side of a mountain. Adventure is
an attitude that is applied to the
daily challenges of life.

Dreams of Nell Shipman

The brightest of all nightscapes is when
a full moon shines on the Selkirks
in the winter.

Dreams of Nell Shipman

"The art of mountaineering is knowing
when to go, when to stay, and
when to retreat."

Ed Viesturs

Dreams of Nell Shipman

All mountains have two stories: the ones we
read about and the ones we create.

North of The Narrows

Add life to your days,
not days to your life.

North of The Narrows

Getting lost is sometimes
the best use of your time.

North of The Narrows

Attitude spells the difference between
an ordeal and an adventure.

North of The Narrows

The goal is to die with memories,
not dreams.

North of The Narrows

Sleep under a cozy blanket of stars,
and your heart will forever
be kept warm.

North of The Narrows

We don't spend time
in the mountains. We invest time
in the wilderness.

Above Eastshore Road

Instead of worrying about the rocks and roots on the trail, just enjoy the moment.

Above Eastshore Road

No-one ever said it would be easy; but they
have promised it would be worth it.

Above Eastshore Road

We don't trip on mountains,
but over molehills.

Chinese Proverb

Above Eastshore Road

"You're braver than you believe, stronger
than you seem, and smarter
than you think."

Christopher Robin

Above Eastshore Road

Don't be afraid to fail.
Be terrified of not trying.

Above Eastshore Road

Fear is temporary, but
regret lasts forever.